Will The
Back By
Monday?

Josephine R. Bay

ISBN: 1-4392-4445-6
ISBN-13: 9781439244456
Library of Congress Control Number: 2009905512
Visit www.booksurge.com to order additional copies.

Dedication

"To Tiffiny – experimenter and optimist.
To Tom who models these traits." J.R.B.

"To three little hairdressers – Emma, Corbin,
and Clay and my patient husband, Lloyd. J.A.S.

School
was over
for another
week. Becky
bent down to pick
up some papers that
had fallen from her
desk. She shoved them
into her backpack and
tried to zip it up, but she
couldn't see the zipper
handle. All day long,
she had tried to keep
her bangs out of her
eyes. They had
been out of
control!

She moved
them to one side, and
they slid right back into her
eyes. She moved them to the other
side, and they slid right back into her
eyes. She ran her fingers through her
bangs, hoping they would stay
on top of her head. They
wouldn't.

3

She searched her backpack for
a ribbon, a hair band, a bobby pin,
anything --even a paper clip -- to keep
her bangs out of her eyes. She couldn't
find one, single, solitary thing to hold
her bangs in place. It was a bad
hair day.

HAT Shoppe

Becky grabbed her
back-pack and headed
home. As she walked
past the grocery store,
Becky looked at her
reflection in the window.
She was sure her bangs
had grown longer since
leaving school.

She walked past the
department store, and
looked at her reflection in
the window. She blew her
bangs away from her face as
she moved closer and closer to
the window. "Oh, goodie!" she
exclaimed, "The hat is still in the
window." Becky's birthday was
just a week away, and when her
mom had asked her what she
would like for her birthday,
Becky told her about the hat.

HAT Shopp

Becky passed Mrs. Graham's house
and said "hi." Mrs. Graham had long,
shaggy hair. Her dog had long, shaggy
hair. "I wonder how they find each other,"
Becky thought to herself as she pushed
her bangs off her face.

She passed Mr. Newland's house and said "hi." He was bald, and so was his dog. "They can always see each other!" she laughed to herself.

When Becky arrived home from school, she went straight to her bedroom for a hair band. She heard Mom say, "Hi, Punkin." Becky hurried into the kitchen and hugged her mom. She had forgotten all about her uncontrollable bangs.

She petted Kitty and fetched him some fresh water. Mom put milk and cookies on the table for Becky.

"Well, tomorrow is a big day for us," said Mom.

"I can't wait," replied Becky. She and her mother were going to make birthday party invitations, and on Monday, Becky would deliver them to her friends at school.

Saturday morning came bright and early. Becky rolled over in her warm, cozy bed. She opened one eye, then another. She could see sunbeams peeking through the shades of her window casting a light on her stickers, colored paper, markers, glue, and glitter strewn across her desk.

"Yippee,
it's Saturday!"
she exclaimed as
she stretched both arms
high above her head. Then
tossing her down-filled quilt
across the bed, she sat up and
dangled her legs and wiggled
her toes. She jumped from her
bed and started to make it, but
she couldn't see the corner of her
sheet. Her hair band had come
off in the night, and her bangs
were hiding her eyes. Becky
knew she had to do something
about them before she and
Mom started making the
invitations.

Becky wondered what
her mom and dad were doing. She
peeked into the kitchen. Mom was singing
to herself while making breakfast. She peeked
into the guest room. Dad was grunting to
himself while hanging the wallpaper.

"Perfect," she whispered.

Becky
went into the
bathroom, pulled
her pink stool up to
the sink, opened the
medicine cabinet door, and
stretched, and stretched
as far as she could to reach
the hair scissors. With her
fingers curled around the
handle, she gently pulled
them off the shelf. "I can
do this myself now. I'm
getting older," she
announced.

Becky combed her bangs
straight down and wet them with
water. She combed her bangs again
and parted them into three sections.
She was ready to start.

Holding some of her bangs between the fingers of her left hand, and taking a deep breath, she picked up the scissors, and, *snip!* Hair fell on her nose. "That tickles," she giggled. She held more bangs between her fingers, and, *snip!* Hair fell on her cheeks. "This is fun," she exclaimed. "Just one more snip and I'll be done," she said as she gathered the last of the bangs between her fingers. *Snip!* Hair fell in the sink.

Becky looked down at all the hair.
Then she looked in the mirror.

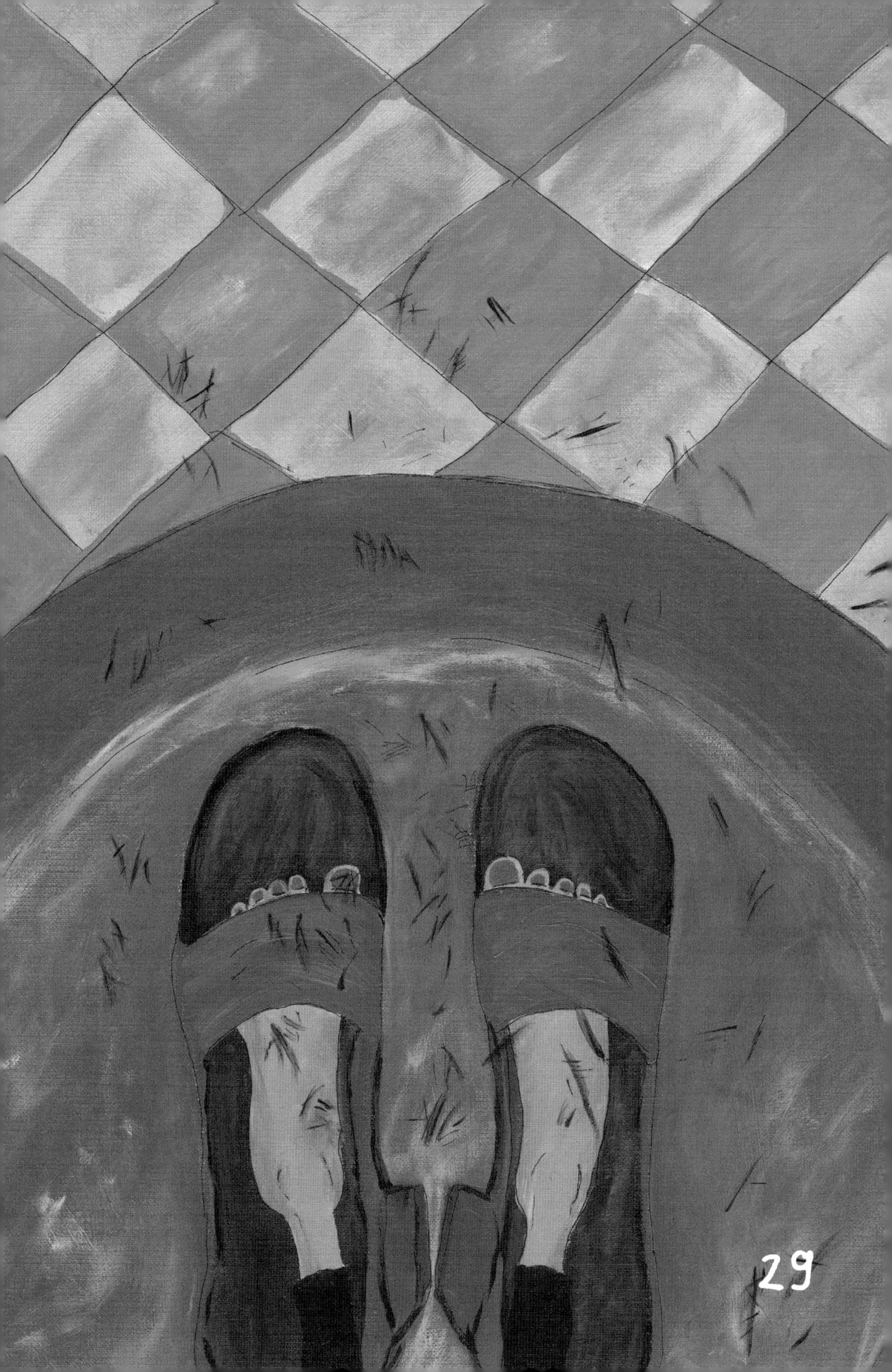

"Hmmm,"
she said as the
corner of her mouth
moved to one side,
"they're crooked!"
She paused for a
moment before
starting again.

She wet down the bangs, and she could see where they weren't even. *Snip! Snip! Snip!* "That should do it." Becky said as she moved closer to the mirror.

"Hmmm, they are still uneven." She wet them down again. This time she decided to cut with her left hand, and hold the bangs with her right hand. *Snip! Snip! Snip!*

When
she looked
in the mirror, she
was horrified. Her
bangs were sticking out
from her forehead. They
were *short, short, short!* She
grabbed her face between
her hands. "Oh, no, what
have I done?" wailed Becky.
She looked at herself in the
mirror again and let out a
blood-curdling scream!
She screamed so loud it
frightened her more
than her very
short bangs.

Kitty jumped off the couch and ran under the bed. Becky's mom and dad were frightened, too. They ran to Becky.

There she
stood on her pink
stool, looking dreadfully,
dreadfully, dreadfully silly
with her new hairdo. Mom and
Dad saw hair on her nose, hair
on her cheeks, and hair on her chin.
They saw hair on the floor, hair on her
stool, and hair in the sink.

Mom and Dad glanced at each other. It
was hard for them not to laugh out loud
as they looked at Becky's short bangs.
Becky couldn't see the smiles on their
faces because her eyes were clouded by
big tears. She blinked, and the tears fell
to her cheeks. "Will they grow back by
Monday?" she sobbed, wondering what
her friends would think when they saw
her new hairdo.

"No my dear, they will not grow
back by Monday" said Mom,
"but they will grow back in a
bunch of Mondays."

"Will they grow this much by Monday?" asked Becky, placing her finger in the middle of her forehead.

"Nope, they won't grow back that much by Monday," replied Dad.

"Will they grow this much by Monday?" asked Becky, placing her finger higher on her forehead.

"Nope, they won't grow back that much by Monday," said Mom.

42

"Will they grow this much by Monday?" asked Becky, placing her finger just a millimeter or two from her bangs.

"Yes, I think they will grow that much by Monday," assured Dad.

"I look just like Mr. Newland's no-hair dog," bawled Becky as she glanced back at herself in the mirror. Becky's bangs wouldn't bother her for a long, long time.

Mom had an idea. "I'll be right back." She returned carrying a box wrapped in colorful birthday paper, tied with a ribbon and bow. "It's an early birthday present," Mom told Becky as she handed it to her. Becky wiped the last of her tears from her eyes and opened the pretty box. Inside nestled between pink tissue paper, was the hat Becky had wanted.

"Oh, Mommy!" exclaimed Becky as she took it out of the box and tried it on.

"Now you can't see my very, very, very, very short bangs," she laughed.

"There's something else in the box," said Mom.

Becky looked
once more. She
found a little packet.
"What's in here?" she asked
as she opened the box. And
there they were; the little pink
bunny rabbit barrettes that Becky
liked.

"They can be a substitute when you're
tired of wearing the hat," offered Dad.

"Oh, I'll wear them together, and
never get tired," replied Becky. She
glanced in the mirror one more time
and thought to herself, *"I like my
new look."* She hugged her Mom.
She hugged her dad. "Let's have
breakfast quick so we can make
birthday invitations for
my friends," Becky said
excitedly.

HAPPY*BIRTHDAY

Made in the USA
Charleston, SC
20 February 2010